Stories
for a
Prince

These fourteen stories are the winning entries from a national schools competition entitled "A Royal Book at Bedtime". Schoolchildren throughout the country were invited to help Britain's 130,000 blind people by writing a sponsored bedtime story for HRH Prince William of Wales. In aid of Blind Care, an appeal of the Royal National Institute for the Blind, the competition was endorsed by television and radio personality Terry Wogan, and sponsored by H. J. Heinz Co. Ltd. Approximately 7,500 children entered the fundraising competition which was one of the most successful promotions ever mounted by RNIB.

A copy of *Stories for a Prince* has been presented to HRH The Princess of Wales for Prince William.

All royalties from the sales of this book will be donated to RNIB and will be used for braille production. *Stories for a Prince* is available in braille from RNIB.

"A Royal Book at Bedtime" was devised and organised by James H. Campbell & Associates (a member of the Campbell Sadler Lohan Group).

Stories
for a
Prince

Hamish Hamilton · London

An appeal of the Royal National Institute for the Blind

The Royal National Institute for the Blind is a national voluntary organisation which exists to help Britain's 130,000 blind people. Services provided by RNIB include rehabilitation for people who lose their sight, physiotherapy training, help for parents of blind babies, schools and nursery schools to give blind children a good start in life, help for blind students through college and university including braille and tape study books, a job-finding service, a talking books library, holidays for blind people and homes for the elderly. Services for blind people cost approximately £15 million per year, half of which comes from voluntary fund-raising, donations and legacies. The RNIB's patrons are HM The Queen and HM Queen Elizabeth the Queen Mother.

First published in 1983
Published by Hamish Hamilton Children's Books
Garden House 57–59 Long Acre London WC2E 9JZ
Copyright © 1983 The Royal National Institute for the Blind
All Rights Reserved

British Cataloguing in Publication Data
Hamish Hamilton
Stories for a prince
I. Title
823′ .914 [J] PZ7
ISBN 0 241 11052 1

Designed by Peter Sims
Typeset by Katerprint Co Ltd, Cowley, Oxford

Originated and printed in Italy by
Arnoldo Mondadori Editore, Verona

Contents

Page

Illustrated by Tamasin Cole

The Little Black Seal

by Anna McKibbin

One day Oliver the Eskimo boy put on his warmest clothes and went for a walk. It had been snowing and the new snow was crunchy under his feet. He was just thinking of going back to his igloo when he saw a little black seal. The seal looked very sad so Oliver decided to try and cheer him up.

"Why are you so sad?" asked Oliver.

"I am sad because the water is frozen over and I cannot catch any fish," answered the seal.

"Perhaps if we thought very hard we might find a way of catching fish," Oliver said hopefully. But even with two people thinking as hard as they possibly could, they could not find a way round the problem.

It was getting colder so Oliver collected some wood and made a fire. The boy and the seal were soon fast asleep.

When they woke up there was a large hole in the ice where the fire had been.

"Look! Look! the fire has made a hole in the ice!" cried Oliver excitedly.

"Now I can go fishing!" cried the little seal and dived through the hole immediately. As quickly as he had dived in he came out again with two fish. Oliver ate one of the fish and the little seal ate the other. The seal was able to fish whenever he wanted and he and Oliver had a fish supper every night.

Illustrated by Heather Buchanan

How Giraffe Got His Long Neck

by Hugo Speer

Long, long ago in a country called Africa, there was born a tiny spotty animal. It was small, had quite long legs and a short neck. It was orange with brown spots. Everyone who saw this little creature called it "Giraffe" because, in their funny language, this meant "Oh Spotty One".

Soon Giraffe grew bigger but he still did not have the long neck which we know him by today.

One day Giraffe decided to set off to explore the world. He came to a place called India and the first person he met was a very naughty man called Evil Abdhulla. He was a nasty wizard who was always casting even nastier spells.

"Hello," said Giraffe happily.

"Get out of my way, you spotty bother, or I'll cast one of my evil spells upon you!"

Poor Giraffe had met the Evil Abdhulla on a bad day because Abdhulla had got out of bed on the wrong side and was in a bad mood.

"I beg your pardon," said Giraffe politely.

"Pardon? Is that all you can say? Pardon? Pah! Because I am in a very bad mood I'm going to cast one of my evil spells on you. From now on – if anyone says 'pardon' – your neck will grow one inch. Hee hee . . ."

And that is just exactly what the nasty man did; he waved his magic wand and left poor Giraffe worrying what to do. Giraffe decided that he must go on with his exploring and quite soon he came to another country called Italy. There he came to a tall man who was walking by.

Giraffe was still sad and worried but, being very polite, he said in a tiny muffled voice: "Hello!"

Of course the Italian gentleman could not know the meaning of what he said. "Pardon Signor?"

Oh no! Poor Giraffe felt his neck growing. What was he to do? He must start being more careful about what he said.

Giraffe carried on with his travels. He came to a large palace where the King and Queen lived. He knocked on the door and was asked inside by the Queen. Giraffe explained sadly to the King and Queen what had happened to him. He was asked to stay to tea.

While they were having tea the naughty King burped and, without thinking, the Queen said: "One hereby grants one the Royal Pardon."

Silly Queen! Giraffe's neck grew again.

"Oh, pardon me" said the silly Queen and Giraffe felt his neck grow still further. He thanked the King and Queen for their hospitality but said he must be going as he didn't want his neck to grow any longer.

He soon came to a big city and Giraffe was fascinated by the tall buildings and so many people. He was about to wish that he had never left home when out of a big shop staggered an Indian man carrying lots of parcels. The man couldn't see where he was going and Giraffe was

too amazed by the buildings to notice anything. They bumped into each other. The worst thing possible was about to happen to poor Giraffe. The Indian man said: "Oh, golly gosh! A THOUSAND PARDONS!!!"

And can you guess what happened? Yes. The unfortunate Giraffe's neck grew and grew and grew until it was so long that he found out that he was a vertigo sufferer.

From that day on the Giraffe has had a very long neck, but he has learnt to stand heights. So if you see a giraffe with a sad look in his eyes, it could well be our friend with a sore throat and no scarf long enough to keep it warm and make it better!

Illustrated by Helen Craig

The Jumping Competition

by Christopher Cooper

The flea, the grasshopper and the jumping jack decided to hold a competition, to see who could jump the highest. They sent out invitations all over the world to come and view this, "Wonderful display of physical agility," as the invitations proclaimed. The king of Mazolia was so impressed that he offered half his kingdom and his daughter's hand in marriage to the winner.

At last the preparations were complete and the big day was here. Banners and bunting had been raised all over the country and there was excitement throughout the land.

The flea was first and he jumped so high that when he came down an hour later he told the judges that he had chatted with the angels in the

clouds and he even produced a golden harp to prove it!

Next went the grasshopper. He crouched down on his haunches and his legs snapped straight. A second later he was soaring through the air so that even the judges with their powerful binoculars couldn't see him. Two hours later he fell to earth into the lap of the Lord Mayor's wife. The grasshopper mumbled an incredible story about flying past the moon, while eating a piece of green cheese which he had broken off the moon as he was flying past.

Next it was the turn of the jumping jack. He twisted his head round at least forty times, lay down on the ground and suddenly he was soaring into the heavens. He wasn't back in time for Christmas and as far as I know the king of Mazolia, his pretty daughter, the judges, the Lord Mayor, the flea, the grasshopper, the tea lady and most of the other guests are still waiting to this day.

Illustrated by Jenny Thorne

Desmond the Dragon-droid

by Pauline Munro

It was Monday morning, and Desmond the dragon-droid had to go to school. Oh how he hated school! All the other little dragon-droids laughed at him just because he had bright yellow wings and a red body, instead of being green all over. Nobody ever shared their aluminium spaghetti and iron nuts with him. If only his big brother wasn't so clever. All he ever heard was, "Daniel did this and Daniel did that!" The little dragon-droid pulled his brown school satchel along the floor. Slump, slump, bump, bump went his bag as he slowly walked to school.

On the way he was passed by many other dragon-droids, but they didn't even look at him and instead blew fire into his face. Desmond tried to blow some back, but all that came was a tiny, tiny wisp of smoke. There was no sign of a brilliant yellow flame. How he wished he could blow fire. Desmond wished he could do many things, but he didn't have the strength – or the courage. The little dragon-droid stretched his wings and with a tear in his eye he walked through the school gates dragging his school bag.

"Stop snivelling, Desmond!" boomed Mr Macpherson. Desmond was standing in the corner with the bright red dunce's cap on. He had tried and tried to blow fire, but he couldn't, and he felt so ashamed

when all the other little dragon-droids laughed at him. There was only one thing Desmond thought he could do – and that was run away. Instead of going home to his mummy, Desmond would go to the wastelands to live alone, where no horrid dragon-droids could giggle at him. Desmond kept his copper-plate sandwiches in his lunchbox and when home-time came, he walked in the opposite direction from home.

"Where are you going, Desmond?" asked the little dragon-droids.

"Just to my Aunt Dot's," said Desmond. As soon as he was round the corner he ran like the wind to the wastelands.

It was nearly night-time and Desmond had eaten his copper-plate sandwiches long ago. He sat against a tree trunk and looked around him.

"It isn't so nice out here after all," thought Desmond. "I wish mummy was with me, then I wouldn't feel so scared," Desmond sighed. The wind was roaring and the moon a yellow circle hanging in the blackness. An owl hooted. Desmond shivered and then some voices cackled and laughed.

"Hello, pretty little droid!" they said, "Come here, come and play, would you like an iron nut?"

"N–N–No thank you," said Desmond and sat there feeling very frightened.

"Come here little droid. Come and play!" they shrieked.

"No, no, go away!!" Desmond shouted, and quite suddenly out came a big puff of fire and the voices instantly went away. "I can breathe fire!" Desmond yelled "I can do it, I can breathe fire!!"

Desmond ran all the way home and his mummy was overjoyed to see him, and told him never, never to run away again, and Desmond never did run away again because he could breathe fire. He became the best fire breather and his skin was a beautiful bright green. Desmond won all the school competitions, and when he grew up, he became teacher of how to breathe fire, and now if any little dragon-droid cannot breathe fire he sends them to the wastelands to stay a night, and then they are able to breathe big, hot, orange, red and yellow flames.

Illustrated by Babette Cole

Nessie, the Lonely Loch Ness Monster

by Nicola Howat

Once upon a time, there was a little monster who lived in a Scottish loch, called Loch Ness. He was a lonely little thing and he was very sad. You see, everybody thought he was a big, frightening monster and every time he swam to the top all the children ran away. Nessie just cried and cried at the bottom of the loch and it got deeper and deeper and deeper.

Down a little path and through some trees lived a small boy called Hamish McSporran. He lived on a small farm called a croft. Hamish's dad told him that there was a monster which lived in the loch. Every day Hamish went down to the loch and tried calling Nessie, saying, "Nessie, Nessie are you big? Are you small? Will I ever see you at all, at all?"

But Nessie never appeared, until, one day, Nessie surfaced. Hamish McSporran was very surprised! He had expected to see a large monster, but what greeted him was very small and what's more looked friendly!

"Hello, I'm Nessie, the Loch Ness monster."

"B . . . b . . . b . . . but I thought you were big and ever so vicious," gasped Hamish.

"So does everyone," groaned Nessie, "and I'm not. Please, will you be my friend? I'm ever so lonely."

Every day Hamish McSporran and his new friend, Nessie (no longer a lonely monster) swam in the loch. Hamish was given free rides across the loch on Nessie's back and every day he said his little rhyme. "Nessie, Nessie, are you big? Are you small? Will I ever see you at all, at all?" Now, however, Nessie always came.

One day Hamish said to Nessie "Who will play with you in the winter?"

"I don't know," he answered, "maybe I should look for another Nessie."

"But I don't think that there is another Nessie. Not in the whole world."

They looked over the shallow side and the cold side, the windy side and the sunny side. They looked everywhere, but still they did not give up. They looked again and again. Shallow side, cold side, windy side and the sunny side, but still they did not find a friend for Nessie.

On the fifth day Nessie gave a monster call and actually heard a Scottish monster's call in reply. He swam as fast as he could towards the call which he decided was definitely a Nessie type call. Then he stopped dead in his tracks. He had forgotten all about Hamish and left him behind. Nessie decided to show his friend to Hamish, but, oh dear! when Nessie looked back he saw Hamish swallowing half the loch. He had seen Nessie swim off and tried to follow him, but he had caught his leg in the reeds and was now struggling for his life. Nessie went to the rescue, but someone had got there first. When Nessie reached Hamish he saw the most beautiful monster in the world.
After Hamish was safely on the bank, Nessie asked Bessie (who was the other monster) to go for a swim and it wasn't long before Nessie asked Bessie to marry him.

They were married the very next day and Hamish threw fish instead of confetti. Hamish often went swimming with them and they all lived happily ever after.

Illustrated by Terry McKenna

The Man With the Golden Hair

by Victoria Southwell

 long, long time ago, there lived an old man on the top of a high mountain. The man was called Old Scrunge. He lived all alone in a cave and grew spaghetti. He ate spaghetti for breakfast, spaghetti for lunch and, believe it or not, spaghetti for tea as well. Despite his age he had long, long golden hair.

One fine morning Old Scrunge got up, did a few press-ups to get his circulation going and looked in the mirror. The sight he saw nearly made him fall over backwards with surprise. There in the mirror was a quite, quite bald man looking back at him!

"My hair!" said Scrunge, "My beautiful golden locks!" With this he fell to the ground with a flump.

After an hour or so Scrunge got over his shock and went to tend his spaghetti trees. As he was doing this, a wide smile spread across his face.

"I've got it, I'll find a special new spaghetti, a golden colour that I can use for my hair," yelled Scrunge. But he knew it would be hard because his spaghetti was thick and the colour of stodgy putty. He knew what he must do. Scrunge packed some spaghetti in a red cloth and set off on his long journey to find a golden spaghetti.

He travelled far and wide, through Cuckoo Land, where he saw the rare pink elephant, the Province of Snores, where everyone sleeps and many, many more interesting lands, but nowhere could he find a type of golden spaghetti.

Old Scrunge was about to give up when he met a mouse on the way.

Old Scrunge poured out his troubles to the mouse who let out a cry.

"Why not paint your spaghetti gold?"

"That's it!" yelled Scrunge, "My dear mouse let me shake you by the hand . . . er paw."

Old Scrunge was again full of confidence and skipped all the way back to his cave in the mountains.

Old Scrunge had a forgotten cupboard right at the back of his cave. It had not been "explored" for at least 50 years! Scrunge knew that somewhere in the cupboard was a tin of gold paint. Scrunge opened the cupboard door and looked for the paint. In the process he found many things including a tuba, a pair of nail clippers, some braces, his only

book and a picture frame. In the end, he found the paint and rushed to his kitchen where he found a knife. He then rushed out to his spaghetti and cut each strand into six thin strips. When he had enough, he rushed back to his cave and painted each strand gold. He then squashed the ends and fixed them to his head.

Scrunge, anxious to show off his new creation, rushed to the nearest town and walked around in a very dignified manner, his hair glistening in the sun. Soon a crowd of old bald-headed men gathered around Scrunge staring in wonder at his hair.

"How did you get your hair to look like that?" asked one toothless old fellow.

"Gather round," said Scrunge, "and I'll tell you."

Scrunge explained to all the old men and everyone started electing him Mayor, President and Councillor all at the same time. During this commotion a great storm was gathering over the heads of the villagers.

Suddenly there was a crack of thunder and the rain poured down, soaking everyone and everything in sight. Unfortunately the paint that Scrunge had used was not waterproof so the paint dripped in little puddles about his feet. Instead of being the hero of the village, he was now the laughing stock. The crowd laughed and jeered as Scrunge made his way slowly and sadly back to his cave. Without even cleaning his teeth he flopped into his bed and knew he would have to stay bald forever.

Illustrated by Frances Elizabeth Livens

Walter Worm

by Andrew Nicholson

Walter Worm always thought he was an ordinary little wriggly worm. But events that day were to prove that he was wrong. He lived in a buttercup plant or rather in amongst its roots underground. His buttercup grew next to the road which led to the palace where the beautiful princess lived.

When Walter was underground he could hear the sounds of travellers passing by above him. He used to wriggly-slide up his burrow to watch them pass by. Some rode in splendid carriages, some in wooden carts, and some just walked enjoying the exercise.

One day, a lazy summer's day, the sort of day that makes the grass look greener and the sky look more blue, Walter was stretched out in the sun playing with his buttercup, making it go backwards and forwards, backwards and forwards when in the distance he heard the sound of an approaching carriage. Walter raised the head end of his body and looked up the road.

The golden carriage of the princess was going to pass right next to Walter's buttercup. Walter slid away from the side of the road, just a little, to be on the safe side. The carriage slowed down. Maybe, Walter thought, because the horse was tired. No, the princess had told the driver to stop near the pretty buttercup, Walter's buttercup.

For a moment he thought his buttercup was going to be picked and put in water in a vase in the palace. The carriage stopped, the princess, and she *was* beautiful, came down the steps onto the grass verge.

"What a pretty yellow flower. I am glad I stopped for a closer look."

Then Walter saw her face change. She suddenly looked sad.

"My shoelace is broken and I'm on my way to the ball." A tiny

glistening tear appeared in the corner of her eye and then ran down her cheek. Walter thought; he thought about the lace-holes in her shoe, he thought how wide his slippery body was and then he spoke.

"Excuse me," he chirped up.

"Hello. What a long slug you are," the princess said to him.

"Er, actually, I'm a worm. A slug is a cousin twice removed," Walter explained. "I'm long enough to lace up your shoe and keep it on tonight."

"Oh! Could you?" she said.

"The pleasure's all mine," Walter said.

The idea worked perfectly, and the princess danced all night. Later on, Walter began to ache a little bit and needed a rest, so the princess sat down a few times to help Walter recover. On the way back to the palace they stopped to dig up Walter's buttercup. This was put in a plant pot on the princess's windowsill. And Walter lived in the soil in amongst its roots.

Whilst Walter lived in the palace he had five waiters all to himself, so, whatever the time of day, Walter could order hoards of ice-cream, lollipops and the purest water. But Walter kept wondering.
He wouldn't be able to hear the travellers' feet knocking on his roof.
So one day he asked the princess if he could have his buttercup back where it was before. The princess agreed to have Walter's buttercup replanted back where it had been. The royal workmen made a house and a garden just for Walter. Now every time a traveller passes he says hello to Walter. At two o'clock on Wednesday afternoons the princess comes to see Walter. Walter gives her tea and biscuits and they live happily together. And Walter has become a legend in that country for helping the princess at the great ball.

Illustrated by Sara Silcock

Dragon Valley

by Robert Edwards

Once upon a time there was a valley where a herd of dragons lived. There were lots of different dragons, small ones, big ones, fat ones, thin ones, red, green, orange and yellow ones. But there was only one blue dragon and instead of fire, he breathed ice.

Illustrated by Priscilla Lamont

The Oak Tree's Secret

by Thomas Kirkham

Thomas decided to go through the churchyard on his way home from school and collect some conkers.

The last lesson was on local history and he was thinking about the story Mrs Healing had told them about Odcombe Church's missing font cover. History was his favourite lesson and he was intrigued by the mystery.

As he was walking along, he decided to stop by the old oak tree. He liked the bark because it had a warm wrinkly feeling. The tree was in a rather overgrown corner of the churchyard and Thomas liked it there because it was peaceful. He often came to sit by the tree to share his secrets with it.

On this particular day, he sat down to eat the apple he had just found in his pocket, and to think about the lesson.

In the eighteenth century, Odcombe Church was reputed to have the

most beautiful font cover in the country. Then it mysteriously disappeared, and ever since, the church font had a plain cover.

Mrs Healing had suggested that the Village School should help the Vicar to raise money to have a new one made. As Thomas was thinking these things, he heard a leafy voice calling to him.

"I know the secret . . . "

He turned around to see if there was anyone there, but there wasn't. Then, as the sunshine peppered the branches, he realised the tree was talking! He jumped up and looked at the tree and to his amazement, he could see through and into the tree, like a television screen.

"What secret? What is it?" Thomas muttered, amazed.

"I know what happened to the font cover," said the tree.

"Golly," said Thomas and the oak began to tell its secret.

"Odcombe Church was well known for its font cover. It was made out of dark oak which had been highly polished and had been carved with great care to show Moses in the bullrushes, and it had a handle made out of the finest gold. Because of the font cover's beauty the Montacute parishioners were jealous. So they decided to sabotage it.

"Now the carpenter came to hear about this and he couldn't bear the thought of all those hours of work destroyed by jealousy, so he decided to take the cover and hide it. He set to work making a false one, but instead of oak he used beech and instead of gold he used brass. They laughed and laughed and when the people of Odcombe found out, they banished the

carpenter from Odcombe and didn't let him explain.

"Now I'm the only one who knows where it's hidden," finished the tree. "Dig by my roots on the west side and you will find the cover," croaked the tree.

So Thomas fetched a spade and dug until he found something hard and dirty. He brushed off some of the dirt and saw something shining brightly. Thomas took it home and his Mum helped him clean it up. It was the font cover!

The next day, Thomas took it to school and the school presented it to the Vicar, who was very pleased. Thomas never told anyone how he got the cover. But anyway, who would have believed him?

Illustrated by Charlotte Voake

Black Paint on Briney

by Sarah Anne Joy

Once upon a time there lived a donkey and he was called Briney. One day Farmer Chig-wig came and gave the donkeys some food and drink. Briney went straight for the water. Gulp! gulp! gulp! He nearly drank it all. When he had finished his tummy was rather full. So he started to lean against the railings but, oh dear! oh dear! Farmer Chig-wig had just painted them black, and Briney himself was white. So what do you think happened? Well, he now looked just like a zebra.

A few minutes later Farmer Chig-wig came to see if his railings were dry, but of course they weren't. When he saw that he had a zebra in his field, he ran to 'phone the zoo-keeper. The zoo-keeper brought his truck and put Briney in. Then he drove off. When he got to the zoo he put Briney among the other zebras in an enclosure.

When Farmer Chig-wig counted his donkeys the next day he found out that he had lost one. And when the zoo-keeper counted his zebras he noticed that he had one too many.

The next day it was sunny for a while, then the sky became black with clouds. Suddenly it started to pour with rain, and the zebras were soaked. All the black paint that had been on Briney washed off. When the zoo-keeper saw that there was a donkey among his zebras he took it to the farm in his truck. As soon as Farmer Chig-wig saw that his lost donkey was coming back he ran to meet it.

Soon everybody was back in their normal places, and they all lived happily ever after.

Illustrated by Vanessa Julian-Ottie

A Postbox in Danger

by Alex McKenna

On the corner of Bradly Road, there stood a little postbox, painted in lovely bright glossy red paint. Percy, for that was his name, was very happy on that corner, where the postman came daily and collected all the letters. In the spring the little sparrows and the house martins would come and sit on Percy's shiny red top, and chat to him all day. He had many friends, like the lady at number thirteen. Mrs Wood came up every Sunday with a letter for her sister in Australia. Even though she had known the address for ten years she still

took the letter from the mouth of the postbox at the last moment to check she had the right address. At first, this annoyed Percy, but over the years he got used to it.

Another of his weekly visitors was the Major. He marched up the road with a long wooden stick and boots which clicked every time he moved.

"Here comes the Major," Percy would say to his bird companions, when he heard the clicks. All the birds flew away as the Major came – he looked rather fierce. Unlike Mrs Wood, the Major posted his letter to his daughter, with no messing. He smartly pushed it in, turned on his heel and marched off home. Sometimes he would give a sharp tap on Percy's top, to show that he was pleased with his work.

Samantha, who was seven, was always late in posting her letter to her pen friend. Just as the postman was about to set off, she would come whizzing up the road on her shiny yellow bike, and pop a pink envelope in the postman's sack. Every time she went past Percy, Samantha beamed at him, with a great big smile.

Percy the postbox was not used just for keeping letters safe. Elderly Miss Summers was so tired by the time she reached the postbox, she had to lean on Percy! You see, she had to walk a mile to reach him since he was the nearest postbox where she could post her letter to Albert, the man she was going to marry.

Of course, Percy knew lots of other people, but these were his most regular visitors. The happy postbox agreed to himself that nothing unusual would ever happen to him.

One day Percy noticed signs of "Keep away. Danger!" being put up on the site of old houses next to him. None of this really worried him, as he thought the houses would be demolished and he would remain on the corner of Bradly Road. But soon an engineer came up, and had a chat with a builder next to Percy.

"That postbox is a bit of a problem," said the builder.

"Hmm, yes. It might have to go," replied the engineer thoughtfully.

"I'll have a word with the Mayor," added the builder and walked away.

All this left Percy terribly worried. Thoughts of big scrap yards and postbox crushers entered his mind. He may have to go, the engineer had said. What if he was right? Percy had stood on Bradly road for fifty years, and he couldn't possibly leave now!

The next day was even more frightening for Percy. The two men came again and held a much more serious conversation.

"I've had a word with the Mayor, and he gave me permission to knock down that postbox if I build a small one in the wall," announced the builder.

"Right, I'll carry on with my plans," answered the engineer, and left. Now that Percy's future seemed settled, he realized he needed help quickly. But from whom?

Just then the Major marched up. He arrived in time to see the builder putting a brown sack over Percy's head.

"Stop!" shouted the Major loudly. "What do you think you're doing?"

"Er . . . the postbox is to be crushed," stammered the builder. The Major looked very angry but marched off with "Don't you worry Percy."

When he came back, the Major had gathered together Mrs Wood, Samantha, Miss Summers and the postman. They were all holding banners saying things like, "Save our Percy!" and "Percy must Live!" By this time the anxious builder had run off to the Mayor, who now came nervously down the street. The Major saluted him stiffly.

"Well now, what's the trouble?" asked the Mayor.

"We hear that Percy is to be demolished, and a horrible flat postbox built in his place!" said the Major.

"I won't be able to lean on it!" cried Miss Summers.

"And we won't be able to sit on it," twittered the angry birds.

"It won't be the right shape," said Samantha sadly. The Mayor, frightened there might be a public disturbance, hummed and haahed. Suddenly, charging up the road came Mr Bush, the owner of the Post Office farther up the road.

"I heard about the protest," he panted, "so I came to say that I badly need a postbox outside my shop!" The Mayor smiled and turned to the Major.

"The solution!" he cried. A cheer went up from the crowd. Percy was saved!